OTTO'S ORANGE DAY

JAY LYNCH & FRANK CAMMUSO

OTTO'S ORANGE DAY

A TOON BOOK BY

JAY LYNCH & FRANK CAMMUSO

AN IMPRINT OF CANDLEWICK PRESS

For Ngoc

–Frank

For Kathleen and Norah

–Jay

Editorial Director: FRANÇOISE MOULY

Book Design: FRANÇOISE MOULY & JONATHAN BENNETT

 Printed in Singapore by Tien Wah Press (Pte.) Ltd.
Hardcover Library of Congress Control Number: 2007941868 ISBN: 978-0-9799238-2-1 (hardcover)
ISBN: 978-1-935179-27-6 (paperback)

13 14 15 16 17 18 TWP 10 9 8 7 6 5 4 3 2 1

www.TOON-BOOKS.com

CHAPTER ONE:

MY FAVORITE COLOR!

Orange was Otto the cat's favorite color.
Without orange things,
the world would be boring.
TOYS

Orange is pretty. It's bold and it's strong!
Now check out this ditty; it's my orange song.
I like orange flowers...
...and I wear orange socks...
...and I built a tall tower...

...of bright orange blocks!
So just give me orange. It's bright and it's pretty.
Just give me orange-
And I'm one happy kitty!
DING DONG
Now, who could that be?

Package for you!
Wow! And it's wrapped in orange!
I wonder what it is.
I wonder who it's from.
Great, an orange lamp! And this note says it's from Aunt Sally Lee!
Dear Otto,
I found this old lamp in a strange little store.
I thought you would like it because it's orange, though you might want to give it a good dusting off.
Love,
Aunt Sally Lee

Good idea! I'll just dust it off...
Huh?
POOF
Greetings, Master!
I am the Genie of the Lamp! Your wish is my command.
What?

You freed me from the lamp; I have to grant you a wish. But each owner gets only ONE wish, so choose wisely.
I get a wish?!!
Now, what orange thing should I wish for? Hmm...
Aha! I've got it!

I wish that *everything* in the world was orange!
Your wish is my command, oh master.
Take a look!
Oh, this is gonna be great!

And there were...
Orange planes and orange cranes.
Orange bats and orange hats.
Orange cars and orange stars.

Orange homes...
...with orange gnomes!
Orange skirts...
...and orange shirts!
Orange clowns in orange gowns!

Orange ducks...
...and orange trucks.
Orange bees...
...and orange trees!
Orange monkeys...
...cows and lizards.

And in the winter, orange blizzards.

CHAPTER TWO:

BE CAREFUL WHAT YOU WISH FOR!

Everything's orange! Everything's great! But now, it's time to eat!
Boy! I could use some lunch. This has been quite an exciting morning.
Let's see what we have today.
Aha! An orange popsicle! Yum!

Otto! Give me that popsicle!
What popsicle?
You can have it for dessert. But first you have to eat your lunch!
Aww, Mom.
Here you go. An orange lamb chop, orange spinach, orange mashed potatoes... Oh—and don't forget to drink your orange milk!

Perhaps some things might be better if they were *NOT* orange.
But orange has to be the best. Let's try the lamb chop.
CHEW CHEW
CHOMP GULP
BLAACH!!
Nope. I was wrong.

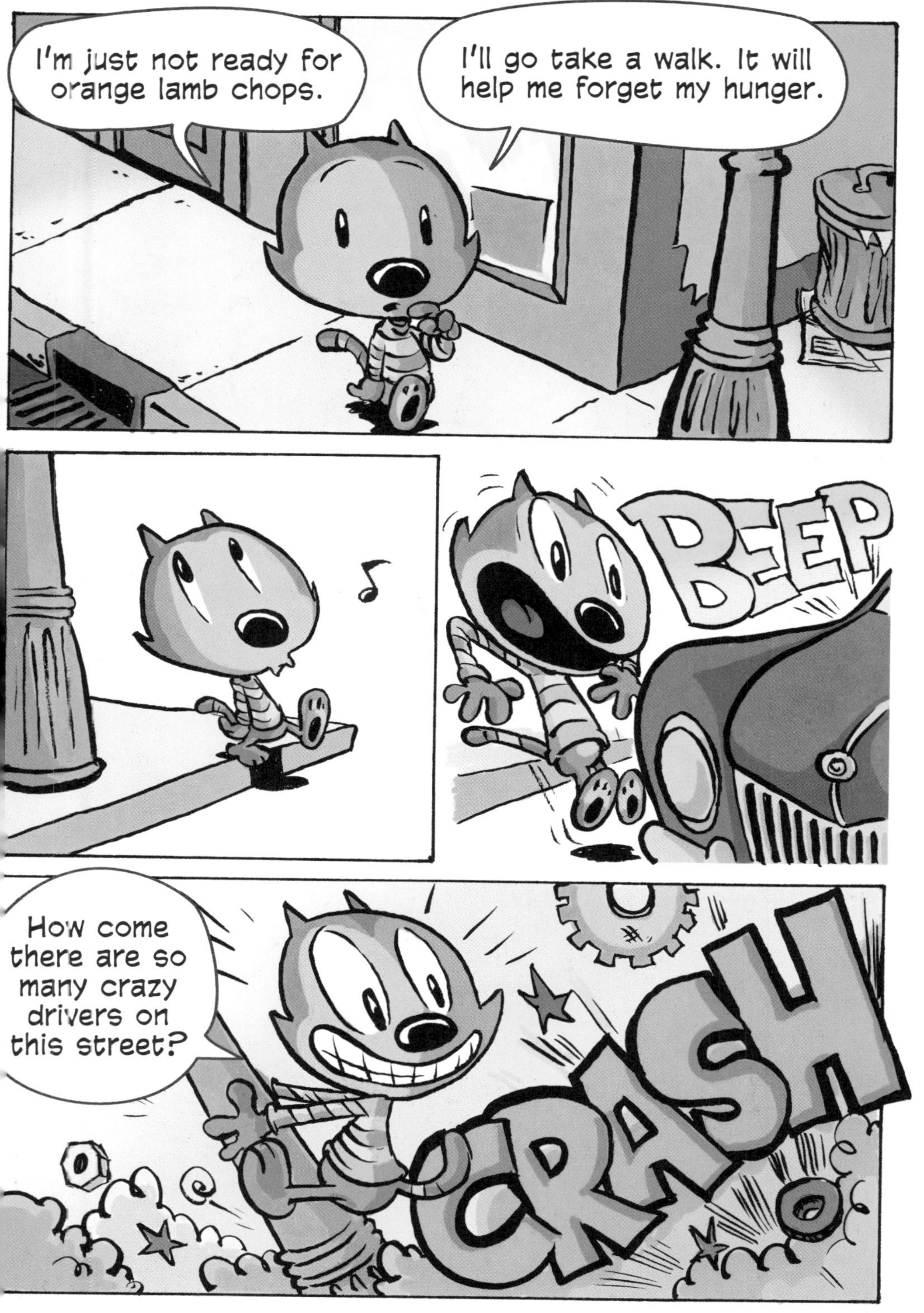
I'm just not ready for orange lamb chops.
I'll go take a walk. It will help me forget my hunger.
BEEP
How come there are so many crazy drivers on this street?
CRASH

Oh, so that's it. All the traffic lights are orange!
That's really dangerous! Hmm...

Hey, Chester! What's up?
Otto! How are you doing?
Say, Chet. How do you feel about this new orange world we're living in?
What do you mean?
Haven't you noticed? Everything is orange now!
What are you talking about?
Well—everything is orange and it's giving me the ***BLUES!***
Giving you the WHAT?

The blues.
What do you mean? What's the blues?
The blues! You know, it makes me sad!
Oh!
You mean you've got the oranges!
-SIGH- I guess so.
Don't worry, Otto. Things will all work out...
But now I gotta go. My mom is making orangeberry pie!
-SIGH- So long, Chet.

ALERT! Be on the lookout for the escaped orange criminal, the Orange Robber.
POLICE
He or she has orange hair...
...and orange eyes...
...and is wearing orange!

The orange bandit could be anywhere.
Or anyone.
It's too dangerous out here. I'm going home.
Hey! Which is my house? They're all orange!
WHEW! Finally— I made it home.
I've got to go to my room and find my lamp.

Oh no! Everything is *ORANGE!* How will I find the lamp?
TOYS
Can you help Otto find the lamp in this clutter?

At last! I've found it!
Now what will I do? The genie only gave me one wish and I used it. Maybe I'll ask Aunt Sally Lee for help.
Aunt Sally Lee? This is Otto. Listen, it's about the lamp you sent me...
OH! I see. Don't worry— I have an idea, and I'll be right over.

CHAPTER THREE:

A NEW WISH

Now we'll see if we can fix things. Here, Otto, take this nickel.
Sure.
I just bought the lamp from you for a nickel. Now on to the rest of the plan.
RUB
RUB
RUB
You again! Sorry, kid, just one wish!
POOF

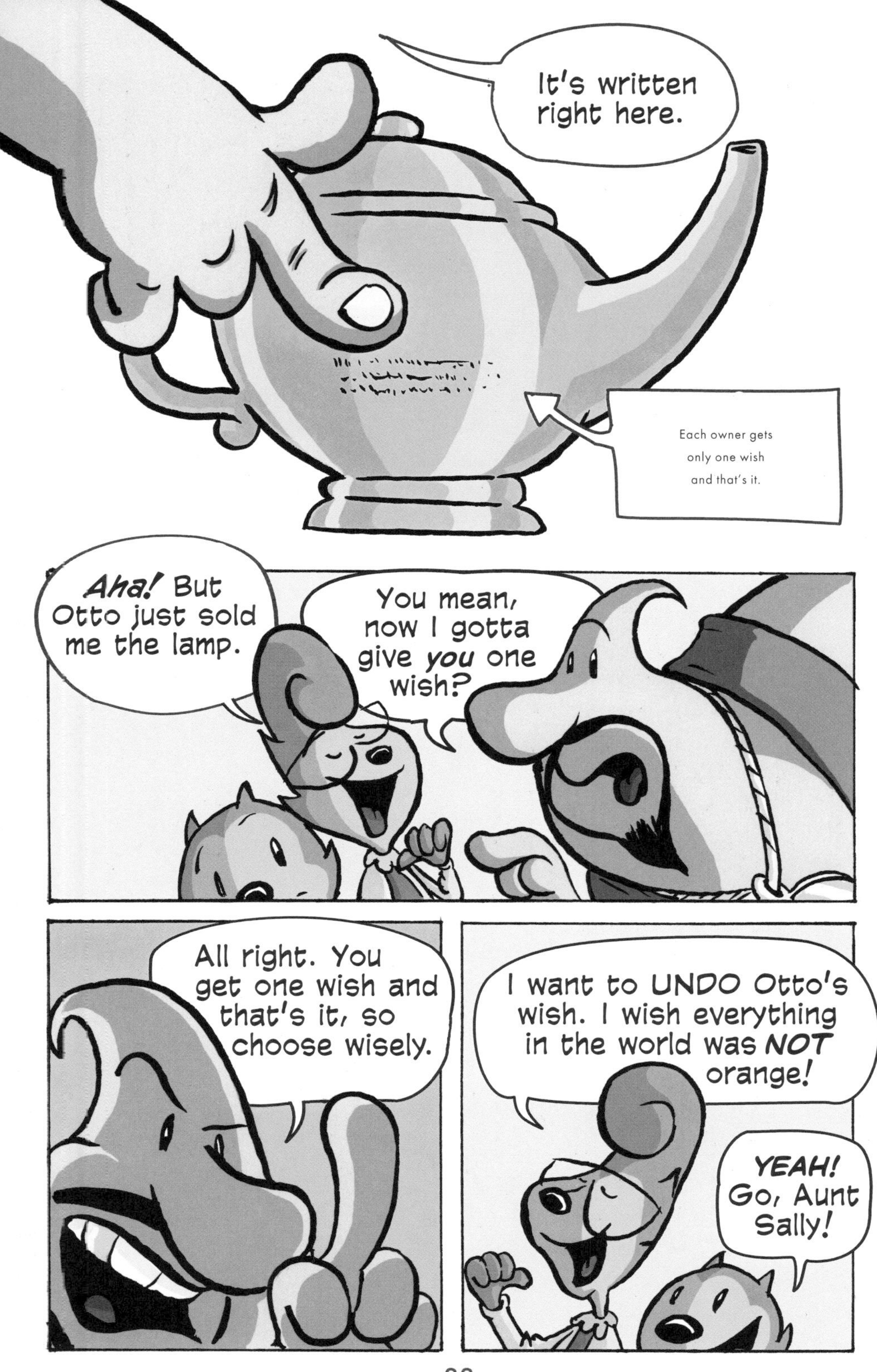
It's written right here.
Each owner gets only one wish and that's it.
Aha! But Otto just sold me the lamp.
You mean, now I gotta give you one wish?
All right. You get one wish and that's it, so choose wisely.
I want to UNDO Otto's wish. I wish everything in the world was NOT orange!
YEAH! Go, Aunt Sally!

As you wish...
Well—I guess everything is NOT orange now, is it?
Now I'm REALLY blue!

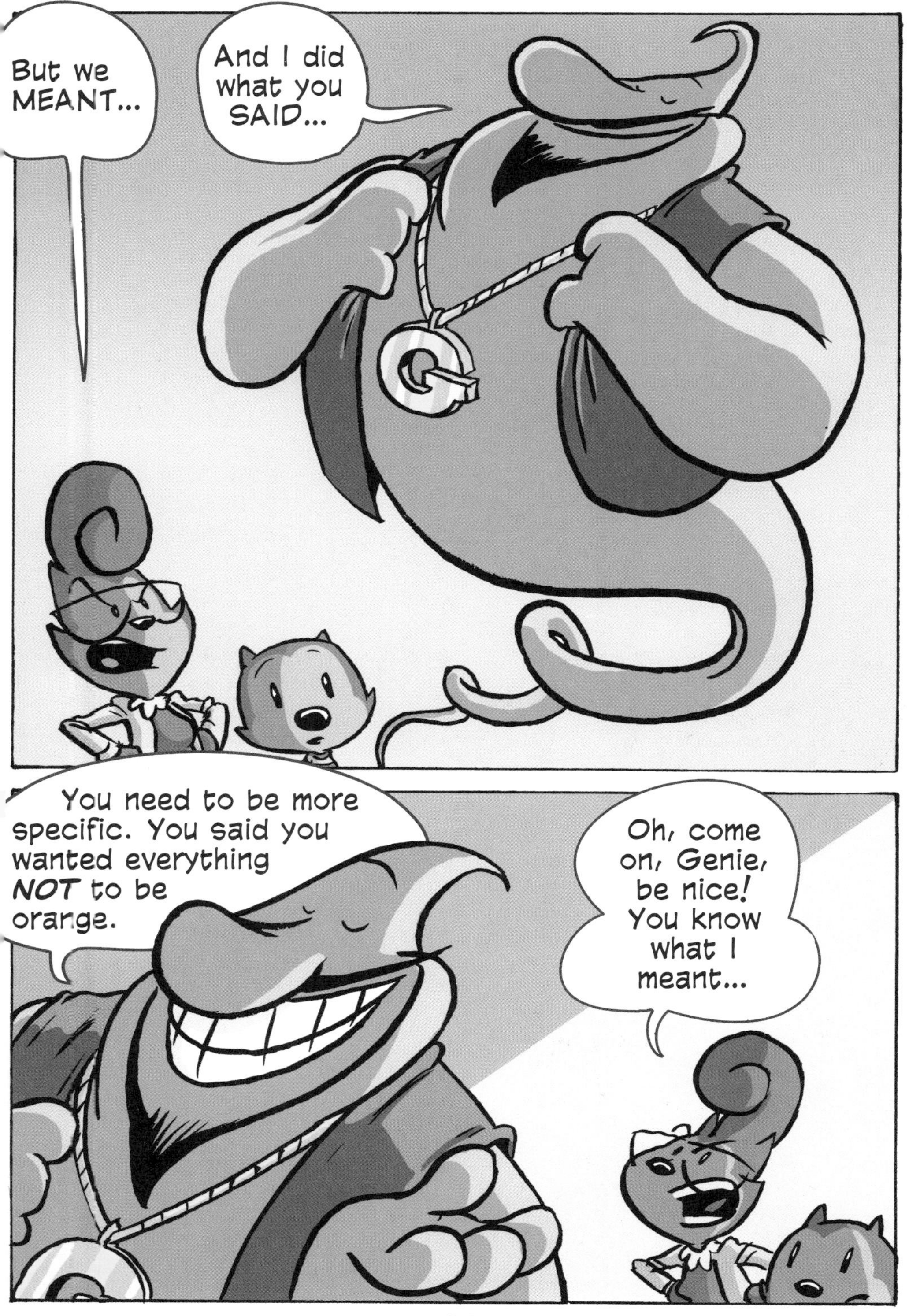
But we MEANT...
And I did what you SAID...
You need to be more specific. You said you wanted everything *NOT* to be orange.
Oh, come on, Genie, be nice! You know what I meant...

All you people do is complain! You are never happy. Humans are SO selfish!
In all the years on the job, did anyone ever think about me?
If someone ever tried to do something for me, I might bend the rules.
You have been in that lamp a long time—When is the last time you ate?
Hmm... 880 years ago?
I have an idea.

Maybe if you were more specific, people could get you what you want.
Whisper... whisper...
Chill out, you two. The problem is as good as solved!
DING DONG

Pizza! Just what I wanted!
But we can't have blue pizza, now can we?
PIZZA PUP
POOF
Smells so good!
Smells so good!
Smells so good!
PIZZA

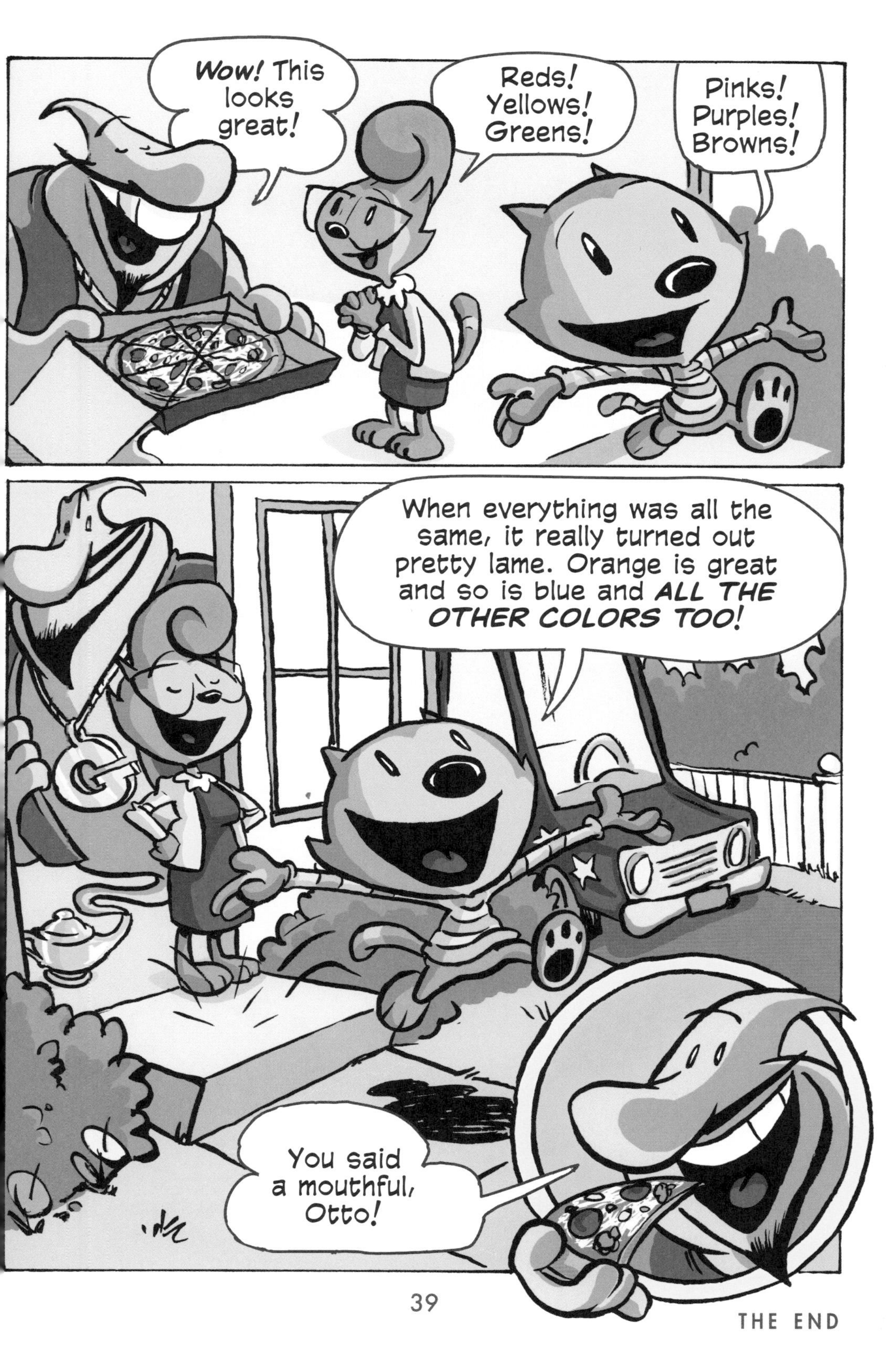
Wow! This looks great!
Reds! Yellows! Greens!
Pinks! Purples! Browns!
When everything was all the same, it really turned out pretty lame. Orange is great and so is blue and ALL THE OTHER COLORS TOO!
You said a mouthful, Otto!
THE END

ABOUT THE AUTHORS

JAY LYNCH, who wrote Otto's story, was born in Orange, NJ (honest, ORANGE, NJ!) and now lives in upstate New York. He is the founder of *Bijou Funnies*, one of the first and most important underground comics of the Sixties, and for many years wrote the weekly syndicated comic strip, *Phoebe and the Pigeon People*. He has helped create some of Topps Chewing Gum's most popular humor products, such as *Wacky Packages* and *Garbage Pail Kids*, and has also composed lyrics for the award-winning rock band The Boogers.

FRANK CAMMUSO, who drew Otto's adventure, lives in Syracuse, New York, where he is the award-winning political cartoonist for the *Syracuse Post-Standard*. He is the Eisner-nominated creator of *Max Hamm Fairy Tale Detective*, selected as one of the Top Ten Graphic Novels of 2006 by *Booklist*, and is the author/illustrator of the *Knights of the Lunch Table* series. His writing has appeared in *The New Yorker*, *The New York Times*, *The Village Voice*, and *Slate*. His favorite color is red.

HOW TO "TOON INTO READING"
in a few simple steps:

Our goal is to get kids reading—and we know kids LOVE comics. We publish award-winning early readers in comics form for elementary and early middle school, and present them in three levels.

FIND THE RIGHT BOOK

Veteran teacher Cindy Rosado tells what makes a good book for beginning and struggling readers alike: "A vetted vocabulary, plenty of picture clues, repetition, and a clear and compelling story. Also, the book shouldn't be too easy—or the reader won't learn, but neither should it be too hard—or he or she may get discouraged."

If you love Otto, look for more of his adventures in "Otto's Backwards Day"

OTTO'S BACKWARDS DAY
by Frank Cammuso with Jay Lynch

The TOON INTO READING!™ program is designed for beginning readers and works wonders with reluctant readers.

TAKE TIME WITH SILENT PANELS

Comics use panels to mark time, and silent panels count. Look and "read" even when there are no words. Often, humor is all in the timing!

3 GUIDE YOUNG READERS

What works?
Keep your fingertip below the character that is speaking.

WHY DID HE FALL DOWN?
WE'LL GET TO THAT. LOOK UP HERE.

DOWN THE STREET.

HA! HA! HA! HA!

HE FELL BECAUSE HE DIDN'T SEE THE BANANA PEEL THAT THE MONKEY DROPPED!

4 LET THE PICTURES TELL THE STORY

In a comic, you can often read the story even if you don't know all the words. Encourage young readers to tell you what's happening based on the facial expressions and body language.

5 GET OUT THE CRAYONS

Kids see the hand of the author in a comic and it makes them want to tell their own stories. Encourage them to talk, write and draw!

Get kids talking, and you'll be surprised at how perceptive they are about pictures.

6 LET THEM GUESS

Comics provide a large amount of context for the words, so let young readers make informed guesses, and don't over-correct. In this panel, the artist shows a pirate ship, two pirate hats, and two pirate flags the first time the word "PIRATE" is introduced.

Here he is!
I'm brave Benny the Pirate!
Benny!